This little piggy . . .

This little piggy . . .

This little piggy . . .

And this little piggy . . .

cried *wee wee wee* all the way home.

This little piggy . . .

This little piggy . . .

This little piggy . . .

This little piggy . . .

This little piggy . . .

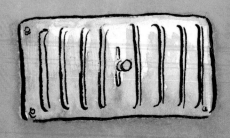

And all the little piggies . . .

First American edition, 1989. Text and illustrations copyright © 1989 by Susan Hellard.
All rights reserved. Originated and published in Great Britain by Piccadilly Press, 1989.
Printed and bound in Colombia. Library of Congress number: 88-23811
Published Simultaneously in Canada
ISBN 0-399-21625-1 First impression

G.P. Putnam's Sons New York